DERELICT

DERELICT

by Alan E. Nourse

John Sabo, second in command, sat bolt upright in his bunk, blinking wide-eyed at the darkness. The alarm was screaming through the Satellite Station, its harsh, nerve-jarring clang echoing and re-echoing down the metal corridors, penetrating every nook and crevice and cubicle of the lonely outpost, screaming incredibly through the dark sleeping period. Sabo shook the sleep from his eyes, and then a panic of fear burst into his mind. The alarm! Tumbling out of his bunk in the darkness, he crashed into the far bulkhead, staggering giddily in the impossible gravity as he pawed about for his magnaboots, his heart pounding fiercely in his ears. The *alarm!* Impossible, after so long, after these long months of bitter waiting— In the corridor he collided with Brownie, looking like a frightened gnome, and he growled profanity as he raced down the corridor for the Central Control.

Frightened eyes turned to him as he blinked at the bright lights of the room. The voices rose in a confused, anxious babble, and he shook his head and swore, and ploughed through them toward the screen. "Kill that damned alarm!" he roared, blinking as he counted faces. "Somebody get the Skipper out of his sack, pronto, and stop that clatter! What's the trouble?"

The radioman waved feebly at the view screen, shimmering on the great side panel. "We just picked it up—"

It was a ship, moving in from beyond Saturn's rings, a huge, gray-black blob in the silvery screen, moving in toward the Station with ponderous, clumsy grace, growing larger by the second as it sped toward them. Sabo felt the fear spill over in his mind, driving out all thought, and he sank into the control chair like a well-trained automaton. His gray eyes were wide, trained for long military years to miss nothing; his fingers moved over the panel with deft skill. "Get the men to stations," he growled, "and will somebody kindly get the Skipper down here, if he can manage to take a minute."

DERELICT

"I'm right here." The little graying man was at his elbow, staring at the screen with angry red eyes. "Who told you to shut off the alarm?"

"Nobody told me. Everyone was here, and it was getting on my nerves."

"What a shame." Captain Loomis' voice was icy. "I give orders on this Station," he said smoothly, "and you'll remember it." He scowled at the great gray ship, looming closer and closer. "What's its course?"

"Going to miss us by several thousand kilos at least. Look at that thing! It's *traveling*."

"Contact it! This is what we've been waiting for." The captain's voice was hoarse.

Sabo spun a dial, and cursed. "No luck. Can't get through. It's passing us—"

"Then *grapple* it, stupid! You want me to wipe your nose, too?"

Sabo's face darkened angrily. With slow precision he set the servo fixes on the huge gray hulk looming up in the viewer, and then snapped the switches sharply. Two small servos shoved their blunt noses from the landing port of the Station, and slipped silently into space alongside. Then, like a pair of trained dogs, they sped on their beams straight out from the Station toward the approaching ship. The intruder was dark, moving at tremendous velocity past the Station, as though unaware of its existence. The servos moved out, and suddenly diverged and reversed, twisting in long arcs to come alongside the strange ship, finally moving in at the same velocity on either side. There was a sharp flash of contact power; then, like a mammoth slow-motion monster, the ship jerked in midspace and turned a graceful end-for-end arc as the servo-grapplers gripped it like leeches and whined, glowing ruddy with the jolting power flowing through them. Sabo watched, hardly breathing, until the great ship spun and slowed and stopped. Then it reversed direction, and the

6

servos led it triumphantly back toward the landing port of the Station.

Sabo glanced at the radioman, a frown creasing his forehead. "Still nothing?"

"Not a peep."

He stared out at the great ship, feeling a chill of wonder and fear crawl up his spine. "So this is the mysterious puzzle of Saturn," he muttered. "This is what we've been waiting for."

There was a curious eager light in Captain Loomis' eyes as he looked up. "Oh, no. Not this."

"What?"

"Not this. The ships we've seen before were tiny, flat." His little eyes turned toward the ship, and back to Sabo's heavy face. "This is something else, something quite different." A smile curved his lips, and he rubbed his hands together. "We go out for trout and come back with a whale. This ship's from space, deep space. Not from Saturn. This one's from the stars."

*

The strange ship hung at the side of the Satellite Station, silent as a tomb, still gently rotating as the Station slowly spun in its orbit around Saturn.

In the captain's cabin the men shifted restlessly, uneasily facing the eager eyes of their captain. The old man paced the floor of the cabin, his white hair mussed, his face red with excitement. Even his carefully calm face couldn't conceal the eagerness burning in his eyes as he faced the crew. "Still no contact?" he asked Sparks.

The radioman shook his head anxiously. "Not a sign. I've tried every signal I know at every wave frequency that could possibly reach them. I've even tried a dozen frequencies that couldn't possibly reach them, and I haven't stirred them up a bit. They just aren't answering."

Captain Loomis swung on the group of men. "All right, now, I want you to get this straight. This is our catch. We don't know what's aboard it, and we don't know where it came from, but it's our prize. That means not a word goes back home about it until we've learned all there is to learn. We're going to get the honors on this one, not some eager Admiral back home—"

The men stirred uneasily, worried eyes seeking Sabo's face in alarm. "What about the law?" growled Sabo. "The law says everything must be reported within two hours."

"Then we'll break the law," the captain snapped. "I'm captain of this Station, and those are your orders. You don't need to worry about the law—I'll see that you're protected, but this is too big to fumble. This ship is from the stars. That means it must have an Interstellar drive. You know what that means. The Government will fall all over itself to reward us—"

Sabo scowled, and the worry deepened in the men's faces. It was hard to imagine the Government falling all over itself for anybody. They knew too well how the Government worked. They had heard of the swift trials, the harsh imprisonments that awaited even the petty infringers. The Military Government had no time to waste on those who stepped out of line, they had no mercy to spare. And the men knew that their captain was not in favor in top Government circles. Crack patrol commanders were not shunted into remote, lifeless Satellite Stations if their stand in the Government was high. And deep in their minds, somehow, the men knew they couldn't trust this little, sharp-eyed, white-haired man. The credit for such a discovery as this might go to him, yes—but there would be little left for them.

"The law—" Sabo repeated stubbornly.

"Damn the law! We're stationed out here in this limbo to watch Saturn and report any activity we see coming from there. There's nothing in our orders about anything else. There have been ships from there, they think, but not this ship. The Government has spent billions trying to find an Interstellar, and never gotten to first base." The captain paused, his eyes narrowing. "We'll go aboard this ship," he said softly. "We'll find out what's aboard it, and where it's from, and we'll take its drive. There's been no resistance yet, but it could be dangerous. We can't assume anything. The boarding party will report everything they find to me. One of them will have to be a drive man. That's you, Brownie."

The little man with the sharp black eyes looked up eagerly. "I don't know if I could tell anything—"

"You can tell more than anyone else here. Nobody else knows space drive. I'll count on you. If you bring back a good report, perhaps we can cancel out certain—unfortunate items in your record. But one other should board with you—" His eyes turned toward John Sabo.

"Not me. This is your goat." The mate's eyes were sullen. "This is gross breach, and you know it. They'll have you in irons when we get back. I don't want anything to do with it."

"You're under orders, Sabo. You keep forgetting."

"They're illegal orders, sir!"

"I'll take responsibility for that."

Sabo looked the old man straight in the eye. "You mean you'd sell us down a rat hole to save your skin. That's what you mean."

Captain Loomis' eyes widened incredulously. Then his face darkened, and he stepped very close to the big man. "You'll watch your tongue, I think," he gritted. "Be careful what you say to me, Sabo. Be very careful. Because if you don't, *you'll* be in irons, and we'll see just how long you last when you get back home. Now you've got your orders. You'll board the ship with Brownie."

The big man's fists were clenched until the knuckles were white. "You don't know what's over there!" he burst out. "We could be slaughtered."

The captain's smile was unpleasant. "That would be such a pity," he murmured. "I'd really hate to see it happen—"

*

The ship hung dark and silent, like a shadowy ghost. No flicker of light could be seen aboard it; no sound nor faintest sign of life came

9

DERELICT

from the tall, dark hull plates. It hung there, huge and imponderable, and swung around with the Station in its silent orbit.

The men huddled about Sabo and Brownie, helping them into their pressure suits, checking their equipment. They had watched the little scanning beetles crawl over the surface of the great ship, examining, probing every nook and crevice, reporting crystals, and metals, and irons, while the boarding party prepared. And still the radioman waited alertly for a flicker of life from the solemn giant.

Frightened as they were of their part in the illegal secrecy, the arrival of the ship had brought a change in the crew, lighting fires of excitement in their eyes. They moved faster, their voices were lighter, more cheerful. Long months on the Station had worn on their nerves—out of contact with their homes, on a mission that was secretly jeered as utter Governmental folly. Ships *had* been seen, years before, disappearing into the sullen bright atmospheric crust of Saturn, but there had been no sign of anything since. And out there, on the lonely guard Station, nerves had run ragged, always waiting, always watching, wearing away even the iron discipline of their military background. They grew bitterly weary of the same faces, the same routine, the constant repetition of inactivity. And through the months they had watched with increasing anxiety the conflict growing between the captain and his bitter, sullen-eyed second-in-command, John Sabo.

And then the ship had come, incredibly, from the depths of space, and the tensions of loneliness were forgotten in the flurry of activity. The locks whined and opened as the two men moved out of the Station on the little propulsion sleds, linked to the Station with light silk guy ropes. Sabo settled himself on the sled, cursing himself for falling so foolishly into the captain's scheme, cursing his tongue for wandering. And deep within him he felt a new sensation, a vague uneasiness and insecurity that he had not felt in all his years of military life. The strange ship was a variant, an imponderable factor thrown suddenly into his small world of hatred and bitterness, forcing

10

him into unknown territory, throwing his mind into a welter of doubts and fears. He glanced uneasily across at Brownie, vaguely wishing that someone else were with him. Brownie was a troublemaker, Brownie talked too much, Brownie philosophized in a world that ridiculed philosophy. He'd known men like Brownie before, and he knew that they couldn't be trusted.

The gray hull gleamed at them as they moved toward it, a monstrous wall of polished metal. There were no dents, no surface scars from its passage through space. They found the entrance lock without difficulty, near the top of the ship's great hull, and Brownie probed the rim of the lock with a dozen instruments, his dark eyes burning eagerly. And then, with a squeal that grated in Sabo's ears, the oval port of the ship quivered, and slowly opened.

Silently, the sleds moved into the opening. They were in a small vault, quite dark, and the sleds settled slowly onto a metal deck. Sabo eased himself from the seat, tuning up his audios to their highest sensitivity, moving over to Brownie. Momentarily they touched helmets, and Brownie's excited voice came to him, muted, but breathless. "No trouble getting it open. It worked on the same principle as ours."

"Better get to work on the inner lock."

Brownie shot him a sharp glance. "But what about—inside? I mean, we can't just walk in on them—"

"Why not? We've tried to contact them."

Reluctantly, the little engineer began probing the inner lock with trembling fingers. Minutes later they were easing themselves through, moving slowly down the dark corridor, waiting with pounding hearts for a sound, a sign. The corridor joined another, and then still another, until they reached a great oval door. And then they were inside, in the heart of the ship, and their eyes widened as they stared at the thing in the center of the great vaulted chamber.

"My God!" Brownie's voice was a hoarse whisper in the stillness. "Look at them, Johnny!"

11

DERELICT

Sabo moved slowly across the room toward the frail, crushed form lying against the great, gleaming panel. Thin, almost boneless arms were pasted against the hard metal; an oval, humanoid skull was crushed like an eggshell into the knobs and levers of the control panel. Sudden horror shot through the big man as he looked around. At the far side of the room was another of the things, and still another, mashed, like lifeless jelly, into the floors and panels. Gently he peeled a bit of jelly away from the metal, then turned with a mixture of wonder and disgust. "All dead," he muttered.

Brownie looked up at him, his hands trembling. "No wonder there was no sign." He looked about helplessly. "It's a derelict, Johnny. A wanderer. How could it have happened? How long ago?"

Sabo shook his head, bewildered. "Then it was just chance that it came to us, that we saw it—"

"No pilot, no charts. It might have wandered for centuries." Brownie stared about the room, a frightened look on his face. And then he was leaning over the control panel, probing at the array of levers, his fingers working eagerly at the wiring. Sabo nodded approvingly. "We'll have to go over it with a comb," he said. "I'll see what I can find in the rest of the ship. You go ahead on the controls and drive." Without waiting for an answer he moved swiftly from the round chamber, out into the corridor again, his stomach almost sick.

It took them many hours. They moved silently, as if even a slight sound might disturb the sleeping alien forms, smashed against the dark metal panels. In another room were the charts, great, beautiful charts, totally unfamiliar, studded with star formations he had never seen, noted with curious, meaningless symbols. As Sabo worked he heard Brownie moving down into the depths of the ship, toward the giant engine rooms. And then, some silent alarm clicked into place in Sabo's mind, tightening his stomach, screaming to be heard. Heart pounding, he dashed down the corridor like a cat, seeing again in his mind the bright, eager eyes of the engineer. Suddenly the meaning of that eagerness dawned on him. He scampered down a ladder, along

12

a corridor, and down another ladder, down to the engine room, almost colliding with Brownie as he crossed from one of the engines to a battery of generators on the far side of the room.

"Brownie!"

"What's the trouble?"

Sabo trembled, then turned away. "Nothing," he muttered. "Just a thought." But he watched as the little man snaked into the labyrinth of dynamos and coils and wires, peering eagerly, probing, searching, making notes in the little pad in his hand.

[Illustration]

Finally, hours later, they moved again toward the lock where they had left their sleds. Not a word passed between them. The uneasiness was strong in Sabo's mind now, growing deeper, mingling with fear and a premonition of impending evil. A dead ship, a derelict, come to them by merest chance from some unthinkably remote star. He cursed, without knowing why, and suddenly he felt he hated Brownie as much as he hated the captain waiting for them in the Station.

But as he stepped into the Station's lock, a new thought crossed his mind, almost dazzling him with its unexpectedness. He looked at the engineer's thin face, and his hands were trembling as he opened the pressure suit.

*

He deliberately took longer than was necessary to give his report to the captain, dwelling on unimportant details, watching with malicious amusement the captain's growing annoyance. Captain Loomis' eyes kept sliding to Brownie, as though trying to read the information he wanted from the engineer's face. Sabo rolled up the charts slowly, stowing them in a pile on the desk. "That's the picture, sir. Perhaps a qualified astronomer could make something of it; I haven't the knowledge or the instruments. The ship came from outside the system, beyond doubt. Probably from a planet with lighter gravity than our own, judging from the frailty of the creatures.

DERELICT

Oxygen breathers, from the looks of their gas storage. If you ask me, I'd say—"

"All right, all right," the captain breathed impatiently. "You can write it up and hand it to me. It isn't really important where they came from, or whether they breathe oxygen or fluorine." He turned his eyes to the engineer, and lit a cigar with trembling fingers. "The important thing is *how* they got here. The drive, Brownie. You went over the engines carefully? What did you find?"

Brownie twitched uneasily, and looked at the floor. "Oh, yes, I examined them carefully. Wasn't too hard. I examined every piece of drive machinery on the ship, from stem to stern."

Sabo nodded, slowly, watching the little man with a carefully blank face. "That's right. You gave it a good going over."

Brownie licked his lips. "It's a derelict, like Johnny told you. They were dead. All of them. Probably had been dead for a long time. I couldn't tell, of course. Probably nobody could tell. But they must have been dead for centuries—"

The captain's eyes blinked as the implication sank in. "Wait a minute," he said. "What do you mean, *centuries?*"

Brownie stared at his shoes. "The atomic piles were almost dead," he muttered in an apologetic whine. "The ship wasn't going any place, captain. It was just wandering. Maybe it's wandered for thousands of years." He took a deep breath, and his eyes met the captain's for a brief agonized moment. "They don't have Interstellar, sir. Just plain, simple, slow atomics. Nothing different. They've been traveling for centuries, and it would have taken them just as long to get back."

The captain's voice was thin, choked. "Are you trying to tell me that their drive is no different from our own? That a ship has actually wandered into Interstellar space *without a space drive?*"

Brownie spread his hands helplessly. "Something must have gone wrong. They must have started off for another planet in their own system, and something went wrong. They broke into space, and they

14

all died. And the ship just went on moving. They never intended an Interstellar hop. They couldn't have. They didn't have the drive for it."

The captain sat back numbly, his face pasty gray. The light had faded in his eyes now; he sat as though he'd been struck. "You—you couldn't be wrong? You couldn't have missed anything?"

Brownie's eyes shifted unhappily, and his voice was very faint. "No, sir."

The captain stared at them for a long moment, like a stricken child. Slowly he picked up one of the charts, his mouth working. Then, with a bitter roar, he threw it in Sabo's face. "Get out of here! Take this garbage and get out! And get the men to their stations. We're here to watch Saturn, and by god, we'll watch Saturn!" He turned away, a hand over his eyes, and they heard his choking breath as they left the cabin.

Slowly, Brownie walked out into the corridor, started down toward his cabin, with Sabo silent at his heels. He looked up once at the mate's heavy face, a look of pleading in his dark brown eyes, and then opened the door to his quarters. Like a cat, Sabo was in the room before him, dragging him in, slamming the door. He caught the little man by the neck with one savage hand, and shoved him unceremoniously against the door, his voice a vicious whisper. "*All right, talk! Let's have it now!*"

Brownie choked, his eyes bulging, his face turning gray in the dim light of the cabin. "Johnny! Let me down! What's the matter? You're choking me, Johnny—"

The mate's eyes were red, with heavy lines of disgust and bitterness running from his eyes and the corners of his mouth. "You stinking little liar! *Talk*, damn it! You're not messing with the captain now, you're messing with *me*, and I'll have the truth if I have to cave in your skull—"

"I told you the truth! I don't know what you mean—"

15

DERELICT

Sabo's palm smashed into his face, jerking his head about like an apple on a string. "That's the wrong answer," he grated. "I warn you, don't lie! The captain is an ambitious ass, he couldn't think his way through a multiplication table. He's a little child. But I'm not quite so dull." He threw the little man down in a heap, his eyes blazing. "You silly fool, your story is so full of holes you could drive a tank through it. They just up and died, did they? I'm supposed to believe that? Smashed up against the panels the way they were? Only one thing could crush them like that. Any fool could see it. Acceleration. And I don't mean atomic acceleration. Something else." He glared down at the man quivering on the floor. "They had Interstellar drive, didn't they, Brownie?"

Brownie nodded his head, weakly, almost sobbing, trying to pull himself erect. "Don't tell the captain," he sobbed. "Oh, Johnny, for god's sake, listen to me, don't let him know I lied. I was going to tell you anyway, Johnny, really I was. I've got a plan, a good plan, can't you see it?" The gleam of excitement came back into the sharp little eyes. "They had it, all right. Their trip probably took just a few months. They had a drive I've never seen before, non-atomic. I couldn't tell the principle, with the look I had, but I think I could work it." He sat up, his whole body trembling. "Don't give me away, Johnny, listen a minute—"

Sabo sat back against the bunk, staring at the little man. "You're out of your mind," he said softly. "You don't know what you're doing. What are you going to do when His Nibs goes over for a look himself? He's stupid, but not that stupid."

Brownie's voice choked, his words tumbling over each other in his eagerness. "He won't get a chance to see it, Johnny. He's got to take our word until he sees it, and we can stall him—"

Sabo blinked. "A day or so—maybe. But what then? Oh, how could you be so stupid? He's on the skids, he's out of favor and fighting for his life. That drive is the break that could put him on top. Can't you see he's selfish? He has to be, in this world, to get anything.

16

Anything or anyone who blocks him, he'll destroy, if he can. Can't you see that? When he spots this, your life won't be worth spitting at."

Brownie was trembling as he sat down opposite the big man. His voice was harsh in the little cubicle, heavy with pain and hopelessness. "That's right," he said. "My life isn't worth a nickle. Neither is yours. Neither is anybody's, here or back home. Nobody's life is worth a nickle. Something's happened to us in the past hundred years, Johnny—something horrible. I've seen it creeping and growing up around us all my life. People don't matter any more, it's the Government, what the Government thinks that matters. It's a web, a cancer that grows in its own pattern, until it goes so far it can't be stopped. Men like Loomis could see the pattern, and adapt to it, throw away all the worthwhile things, the love and beauty and peace that we once had in our lives. Those men can get somewhere, they can turn this life into a climbing game, waiting their chance to get a little farther toward the top, a little closer to some semblance of security—"

"Everybody adapts to it," Sabo snapped. "They have to. You don't see me moving for anyone else, do you? I'm for *me*, and believe me I know it. I don't give a hang for you, or Loomis, or anyone else alive—just me. I want to stay alive, that's all. You're a dreamer, Brownie. But until you pull something like this, you can learn to stop dreaming if you want to—"

"No, no, you're wrong—oh, you're horribly wrong, Johnny. Some of us *can't* adapt, we haven't got what it takes, or else we have something else in us that won't let us go along. And right there we're beat before we start. There's no place for us now, and there never will be." He looked up at the mate's impassive face. "We're in a life where we don't belong, impounded into a senseless, never-ending series of fights and skirmishes and long, lonely waits, feeding this insane urge of the Government to expand, out to the planets, to the stars, farther and farther, bigger and bigger. We've got to go, seeking

17

newer and greater worlds to conquer, with nothing to conquer them with, and nothing to conquer them for. There's life somewhere else in our solar system, so it must be sought out and conquered, no matter what or where it is. We live in a world of iron and fear, and there was no place for me, and others like me, *until this ship came—*"

Sabo looked at him strangely. "So I was right. I read it on your face when we were searching the ship. I knew what you were thinking...." His face darkened angrily. "You couldn't get away with it, Brownie. Where could you go, what could you expect to find? You're talking death, Brownie. Nothing else—"

"No, no. Listen, Johnny." Brownie leaned closer, his eyes bright and intent on the man's heavy face. "The captain has to take our word for it, until he sees the ship. Even then he couldn't tell for sure—I'm the only drive engineer on the Station. We have the charts, we could work with them, try to find out where the ship came from; I already have an idea of how the drive is operated. Another look and I could make it work. Think of it, Johnny! What difference does it make where we went, or what we found? You're a misfit, too, you know that—this coarseness and bitterness is a shell, if you could only see it, a sham. You don't really believe in this world we're in—who cares where, if only we could go, get away? Oh, it's a chance, the wildest, freak chance, but we could take it—"

"If only to get away from *him,*" said Sabo in a muted voice. "Lord, how I hate him. I've seen smallness and ambition before—pettiness and treachery, plenty of it. But that man is our whole world knotted up in one little ball. I don't think I'd get home without killing him, just to stop that voice from talking, just to see fear cross his face one time. But if we took the ship, it would break him for good." A new light appeared in the big man's eyes. "He'd be through, Brownie. Washed up."

"And we'd be *free—*"

Sabo's eyes were sharp. "What about the acceleration? It killed those that came in the ship."

18

"But they were so frail, so weak. Light brittle bones and soft jelly. Our bodies are stronger, we could stand it."

Sabo sat for a long time, staring at Brownie. His mind was suddenly confused by the scope of the idea, racing in myriad twirling fantasies, parading before his eyes the long, bitter, frustrating years, the hopelessness of his own life, the dull aching feeling he felt deep in his stomach and bones each time he set back down on Earth, to join the teeming throngs of hungry people. He thought of the rows of drab apartments, the thin faces, the hollow, hunted eyes of the people he had seen. He knew that that was why he was a soldier—because soldiers ate well, they had time to sleep, they were never allowed long hours to think, and wonder, and grow dull and empty. But he knew his life had been barren. The life of a mindless automaton, moving from place to place, never thinking, never daring to think or speak, hoping only to work without pain each day, and sleep without nightmares.

And then, he thought of the nights in his childhood, when he had lain awake, sweating with fear, as the airships screamed across the dark sky above, bound he never knew where; and then, hearing in the far distance the booming explosion, he had played that horrible little game with himself, seeing how high he could count before he heard the weary, plodding footsteps of the people on the road, moving on to another place. He had known, even as a little boy, that the only safe place was in those bombers, that the place for survival was in the striking armies, and his life had followed the hard-learned pattern, twisting him into the cynical mold of the mercenary soldier, dulling the quick and clever mind, drilling into him the ways and responses of order and obey, stripping him of his heritage of love and humanity. Others less thoughtful had been happier; they had succeeded in forgetting the life they had known before, they had been able to learn easily and well the lessons of the repudiation of the rights of men which had crept like a blight through the world. But Sabo, too, was a misfit, wrenched into a mold he could not fit. He

19

had sensed it vaguely, never really knowing when or how he had built the shell of toughness and cynicism, but also sensing vaguely that it was built, and that in it he could hide, somehow, and laugh at himself, and his leaders, and the whole world through which he plodded. He had laughed, but there had been long nights, in the narrow darkness of spaceship bunks, when his mind pounded at the shell, screaming out in nightmare, and he had wondered if he had really lost his mind.

His gray eyes narrowed as he looked at Brownie, and he felt his heart pounding in his chest, pounding with a fury that he could no longer deny. "It would have to be fast," he said softly. "Like lightning, tonight, tomorrow—very soon."

"Oh, yes, I know that. But we *can* do it—"

"Yes," said Sabo, with a hard, bitter glint in his eyes. "Maybe we can."

*

The preparation was tense. For the first time in his life, Sabo knew the meaning of real fear, felt the clinging aura of sudden death in every glance, every word of the men around him. It seemed incredible that the captain didn't notice the brief exchanges with the little engineer, or his own sudden appearances and disappearances about the Station. But the captain sat in his cabin with angry eyes, snapping answers without even looking up. Still, Sabo knew that the seeds of suspicion lay planted in his mind, ready to burst forth with awful violence at any slight provocation. As he worked, the escape assumed greater and greater proportions in Sabo's mind; he knew with increasing urgency and daring that nothing must stop him. The ship was there, the only bridge away from a life he could no longer endure, and his determination blinded him to caution.

Primarily, he pondered over the charts, while Brownie, growing hourly more nervous, poured his heart into a study of his notes and sketches. A second look at the engines was essential; the excuse he concocted for returning to the ship was recklessly slender, and Sabo spent a grueling five minutes dissuading the captain from accompanying him. But the captain's eyes were dull, and he walked his cabin, sunk in a gloomy, remorseful trance.

The hours passed, and the men saw, in despair, that more precious, dangerous hours would be necessary before the flight could be attempted. And then, abruptly, Sabo got the call to the captain's cabin. He found the old man at his desk, regarding him with cold eyes, and his heart sank. The captain motioned him to a seat, and then sat back, lighting a cigar with painful slowness. "I want you to tell me," he said in a lifeless voice, "exactly what Brownie thinks he's doing."

Sabo went cold. Carefully he kept his eyes on the captain's face. "I guess he's nervous," he said. "He doesn't belong on a Satellite Station. He belongs at home. The place gets on his nerves."

"I didn't like his report."

"I know," said Sabo.

The captain's eyes narrowed. "It was hard to believe. Ships don't just happen out of space. They don't wander out interstellar by accident, either." An unpleasant smile curled his lips. "I'm not telling you anything new. I wouldn't want to accuse Brownie of lying, of course—or you either. But we'll know soon. A patrol craft will be here from the Triton supply base in an hour. I signaled as soon as I had your reports." The smile broadened maliciously. "The patrol craft will have experts aboard. Space drive experts. They'll review your report."

"An hour—"

The captain smiled. "That's what I said. In that hour, you could tell me the truth. I'm not a drive man, I'm an administrator, and organizer and director. You're the technicians. The truth now could save you much unhappiness—in the future."

Sabo stood up heavily. "You've got your information," he said with a bitter laugh. "The patrol craft will confirm it."

DERELICT

The captain's face went a shade grayer. "All right," he said. "Go ahead, laugh. I told you, anyway."

Sabo didn't realize how his hands were trembling until he reached the end of the corridor. In despair he saw the plan crumbling beneath his feet, and with the despair came the cold undercurrent of fear. The patrol would discover them, disclose the hoax. There was no choice left—ready or not, they'd *have* to leave.

Quickly he turned in to the central control room where Brownie was working. He sat down, repeating the captain's news in a soft voice.

"An *hour*! But how can we—"

"We've *got* to. We can't quit now, we're dead if we do."

Brownie's eyes were wide with fear. "But can't we stall them, somehow? Maybe if we turned on the captain—"

"The crew would back him. They wouldn't dare go along with us. We've got to run, nothing else." He took a deep breath. "Can you control the drive?"

Brownie stared at his hands. "I—I think so. I can only try."

"You've got to. It's now or never. Get down to the lock, and I'll get the charts. Get the sleds ready."

He scooped the charts from his bunk, folded them carefully and bound them swiftly with cord. Then he ran silently down the corridor to the landing port lock. Brownie was already there, in the darkness, closing the last clamps on his pressure suit. Sabo handed him the charts, and began the laborious task of climbing into his own suit, panting in the darkness.

And then the alarm was clanging in his ear, and the lock was flooded with brilliant light. Sabo stopped short, a cry on his lips, staring at the entrance to the control room.

The captain was grinning, a nasty, evil grin, his eyes hard and humorless as he stood there flanked by three crewmen. His hand gripped an ugly power gun tightly. He just stood there, grinning, and his voice was like fire in Sabo's ears. "Too bad," he said softly. "You

22

almost made it, too. Trouble is, two can't keep a secret. Shame, Johnny, a smart fellow like you. I might have expected as much from Brownie, but I thought you had more sense—"

Something snapped in Sabo's mind, then. With a roar, he lunged at the captain's feet, screaming his bitterness and rage and frustration, catching the old man's calves with his powerful shoulders. The captain toppled, and Sabo was fighting for the power gun, straining with all his might to twist the gun from the thin hand, and he heard his voice shouting, "Run! Go, Brownie, make it go!"

The lock was open, and he saw Brownie's sled nose out into the blackness. The captain choked, his face purple. "Get him! Don't let him get away!"

The lock clanged, and the screens showed the tiny fragile sled jet out from the side of the Station, the small huddled figure clinging to it, heading straight for the open port of the gray ship. "Stop him! The guns, you fools, the guns!"

The alarm still clanged, and the control room was a flurry of activity. Three men snapped down behind the tracer-guns, firing without aiming, in a frenzied attempt to catch the fleeing sled. The sled began zig-zagging, twisting wildly as the shells popped on either side of it. The captain twisted away from Sabo's grip with a roar, and threw one of the crewmen to the deck, wrenching the gun controls from his hands. "Get the big ones on the ship! Blast it! If it gets away you'll all pay."

Suddenly the sled popped into the ship's port, and the hatch slowly closed behind it. Raving, the captain turned the gun on the sleek, polished hull plates, pressed the firing levels on the war-head servos. Three of them shot out from the Satellite, like deadly bugs, careening through the intervening space, until one of them struck the side of the gray ship, and exploded in purple fury against the impervious hull. And the others nosed into the flame, and passed on through, striking nothing.

DERELICT

Like the blinking of a light, the alien ship had throbbed, and jerked, and was gone.

With a roar the captain brought his fist down on the hard plastic and metal of the control panel, kicked at the sheet of knobs and levers with a heavy foot, his face purple with rage. His whole body shook as he turned on Sabo, his eyes wild. "You let him get away! It was your fault, yours! But *you* won't get away! I've got you, and you'll pay, do you hear that?" He pulled himself up until his face was bare inches from Sabo's, his teeth bared in a frenzy of hatred. "Now we'll see who'll laugh, my friend. You'll laugh in the death chamber, if you can still laugh by then!" He turned to the men around him. "Take him," he snarled. "Lock him in his quarters, and guard him well. And while you're doing it, take a good look at him. See how he laughs now."

They marched him down to his cabin, stunned, still wondering what had happened. Something had gone in his mind in that second, something that told him that the choice had to be made, instantly. Because he knew, with dull wonder, that in that instant when the lights went on he could have stopped Brownie, could have saved himself. He could have taken for himself a piece of the glory and promotion due to the discoverers of an Interstellar drive. But he had also known, somehow, in that short instant, that the only hope in the world lay in that one nervous, frightened man, and the ship which could take him away.

And the ship was gone. That meant the captain was through. He'd had his chance, the ship's coming had given him his chance, and he had muffed it. Now he, too, would pay. The Government would not be pleased that such a ship had leaked through his fingers. Captain Loomis was through.

And him? Somehow, it didn't seem to matter any more. He had made a stab at it, he had tried. He just hadn't had the luck. But he knew there was more to that. Something in his mind was singing, some deep feeling of happiness and hope had crept into his mind, and

24

he couldn't worry about himself any more. There was nothing more for him; they had him cold. But deep in his mind he felt a curious satisfaction, transcending any fear and bitterness. Deep in his heart, he knew that *one* man had escaped.

And then he sat back and laughed.

www.ingramcontent.com/pod-product-compliance
Lightning Source LLC
Chambersburg PA
CBHW050921120626
46552CB00004B/1689